THE RUNNER

Amanda Brown

Series Editor
Neville Grant

LONGMAN

Longman Group UK Limited,
Longman House, Burnt Mill, Harlow,
Essex CM20 2JE, England
and associated companies throughout the world

First published 1993
Second impression 1993

Set in 12/15pt Times

Produced by Longman Singapore Publishers Pte Ltd
Printed in Singapore

ISBN 0 582 21749 0

Illustrated by Steve Jobson

Kgatlhanang ran around the track alone. The other runners were far behind her. She ran easily, listening to the sound of her running shoes – *crunch, crunch, crunch, crunch.*

The school running track was around the edge of the playing field. It was made of hard, dry earth, but there was always a lot of loose sand and grit on the surface. The rubber soles of her running shoes crunched against the track in a steady rhythm, like the beat of a drum. It was a fast, strong beat. Kgatlhanang loved running. The earth seemed to move backwards under her feet as she speeded up. She crossed the finishing line with a smile.

Kgatlhanang lived in a small village about 15 kilometres to the north of Kanye. She went to the Community Junior

School in Kanye itself. She got a lift to Kanye every morning with her neighbour, Mr Leepile. He had a small, red pick-up truck, or bakkie, as they were known. She did not travel home with Mr Leepile. Kgatlhanang always stayed for the athletics practices in the afternoons and she had her own special way of getting home afterwards.

"Well done, Kgatlhanang!" said Mr Sebele, the PE teacher. "First in the girls' 3000 metres race." He checked the time on his stopwatch and looked at the list of results on his clipboard. "It's an excellent time too." He smiled at her. "You're the fastest thing on two legs around here."

It was quite true. She was the best long distance runner in the school. Kgatlhanang found it easy to run 3000 metres.

She walked back across the playing field towards the school buildings. The sun was already low in the sky. The runners had kicked up a lot of dust from the track. The late afternoon sunshine mixed with the dust to form a bright cloud around her. She collected her rucksack from her locker. It contained the brown school dress she wore during the day, her school shoes and her homework. She was wearing a tee-shirt and a pair of shorts. Other pupils changed back into their uniforms to walk home. Kgatlhanang always wore her shorts and tee-shirt for the journey home, but she did not walk – she ran. She put the rucksack on her back and tightened the strap around her waist. Then she set off.

The school was nearly empty at this time of day. Her running shoes made a loud noise on the smooth, cement

floors as she ran through the corridors. Two of her friends were walking slowly ahead, talking to each other. Kgatlhanang ran past them.

"Bye, you two," she said. "See you tomorrow."

"Bye, Kgatlhanang," they called after her. "At the speed you're going, you'll get to tomorrow before us!"

Their laughing voices were already far behind her. Kgatlhanang ran out of the school and up the road, through the village. She passed people walking and people pushing wheelbarrows full of water containers, on their way to the standpipe. She ran past donkey carts, which rolled along slowly. The carts were filled with firewood and the donkeys worked hard to pull them.

Only the cars and minibuses were faster than Kgatlhanang. They went past her, sounding their horns.

But she kept out of their way. She ran on the dirt at the side of the road. Sometimes she had to run around a parked car or a roadside stall, selling fruit. She waved at people she knew, but she never stopped.

When she reached the Hillgate butchery, she turned right along a sandy track. There were fewer cars on this track. There were fewer houses and huts too. She ran past the last hut and saw smoke rising from a fire in the yard. There were 15 kilometres of bush between Kgatlhanang and the fire in her own yard.

Kgatlhanang chose to run home. Mr Sebele was delighted that she did so much extra training in this way, but she had decided to do it herself. She *wanted* to run. She had been very tired, the first time she had run all the way home. Then she had done it again and again. Each time she ran home, it

got easier. She knew that if she kept on running, she would get better and better. She wanted to be a famous runner when she grew up. She wanted to run for Botswana one day.

Kgatlhanang left Kanye behind. The noises of people and their machines stopped. Instead, the sounds of the bush were all around her. She had heard these sounds every day of her life. They were the same sounds Kgatlhanang's ancestors had heard as they went home in the evenings. The crickets were clicking loudly. It was difficult to believe that such a noise came from such small insects. It was impossible to see the crickets. So it seemed as if the air itself was making the noise, as it cooled down after the heat of the day. A Cape Turtle Dove landed in a nearby tree and began to sing. "Ku-KOORR-ru, ku-KOORR-ru, ku-KOORR-ru," sang the bird. To Kgatlhanang it seemed to be singing, "Run FASTer, run FASTer, run FASTer!" She smiled and speeded up a bit.

Kgatlhanang's running shoes sank slightly in the soft sand. It was very dry. No rain had fallen for months and all the grass was pale yellow. Even the aloes looked brown and thirsty. Some of the thorn trees still had green leaves. Their thorns were long and dangerous. Kgatlhanang was careful she did not run into them.

She ran on and on; up a hill, down into a valley and up the other side. The shadows grew longer and longer as the sun got lower in the sky. The track twisted through the bush, like a snake. Kgatlhanang ran along it without stopping. She knew every twist and turn of the track. She liked to think about things as she ran.

She thought about school. She made a list in her mind of all the homework she had to do. Then she started to think about the Social Studies project they were doing. She wondered if Leatile would be there to help the next day. She liked Leatile. He was not a runner; he played basketball. He was a tall boy and the best player on the basketball team. Leatile was a likeable, funny boy. He used to tease Kgatlhanang about her running; he called her 'Lightning-Boots,' or 'Quick-Foot,' or 'Super-Shoes'. But she didn't mind. She thought about Leatile and smiled as she ran.

There was a long, narrow hill halfway between Kanye and Kgatlhanang's home. The area around the hill was rocky and difficult to run through. The track went up one end of the hill, along the top and down the far end. Kgatlhanang looked forward to this part of the journey. The climb to the top of the hill was quite steep, but it was good to reach the top and see the track stretching away in front of her, straight as an arrow. It felt good to stretch her legs and run quickly down the straight track.

When she got to the top, she could see someone else running ahead of her along the straight track. It was a girl; she was small and slender. She wore a short, leather skirt and she was running barefoot. Kgatlhanang was puzzled. She had not seen anyone join the track on her way up the hill. Who was this girl? Kgatlhanang did not think she knew her, although she couldn't see the girl's face. Kgatlhanang decided to catch up with her and find out.

The wind whistled past her ears as she ran along. She went faster and faster, but the girl was still far ahead. She could see the girl's heels glowing in the light of the setting sun as she kicked up a cloud of dust. Kgatlhanang realised, to her surprise, that the gap between them was getting bigger. The other girl was also speeding up and she was faster than Kgatlhanang! No one else from school was faster than Kgatlhanang. So who was she? The girl had nearly reached the end of the track along the hilltop. As she reached the edge of the hilltop, she looked back over her shoulder. For a moment, Kgatlhanang saw her face. Kgatlhanang was surprised, for she saw a look of terror on the strange girl's face. Why was the girl so frightened, she wondered? She wanted to call out to her, but the girl had disappeared down the side of the hill.

"Hey! Don't go! Wait for me!" shouted Kgatlhanang. She too reached the edge of the hilltop and stopped. She looked down the track, expecting to see the girl. But there was no one there.

Kgatlhanang looked all around. There was no sign of anyone. The sun was already halfway down. It was a glowing, red ball, half hidden by the trees. Soon it would be dark. Kgatlhanang had no more time to look for the strange girl. She hurried down the steep track and ran on. She frowned as she ran, because she was still puzzled.

When Kgatlhanang reached the last hill of her journey, the bush was covered in darkness. Where the sun had set, the sky was red. A thin new moon was up there in the red sky.

The moon seemed to be smiling at Kgatlhanang. She heard her little brother calling to her and saw the bright fire in their yard. She was glad to be home.

The next day was a busy one. As usual, Kgatlhanang got a lift into Kanye with Mr Leepile. At school, she and some friends worked through the lunch hour with Mrs Maswabe, their class teacher. Leatile was there too.

"The Speed Queen of Kanye!" he said with a smile, when he saw Kgatlhanang.

"The Boy Magic of basketball!" she teased back. They both laughed. "Anyway," said Kgatlhanang, "last night I saw a girl who is faster than I am."

"Impossible!" said Leatile. "Hey, are you serious? Who is she?" Then Mrs Maswabe came in and they had to stop talking and listen to her.

In Social Studies they were doing a history project. They were trying to finish a display. There would be visitors in school for sports day at the weekend and they wanted to decorate the place. All the maps, paintings, accounts and stories had to be finished carefully. Then they had to be stuck onto sheets of coloured paper, ready to be displayed. The display was for the walls of the reception area, outside the Headmistress's office.

The display was about the movement of the Kololo people through Botswana in the early nineteenth century. The Kololo were people from the Drakensberg area of South Africa. They migrated to Botswana in search of cattle and rich grazing land. They were fierce warriors, trained in some of Shaka Zulu's fighting methods. They defeated many of the different Tswana peoples.

In the afternoon, Kgatlhang changed into her shorts, tee-shirt and running shoes. She was late for the athletics practice, because she had stayed in the classrom talking to Leatile. He had suggested lots of funny, silly ideas for catching the mysterious runner. Kgatlhanang had laughed so much, she had forgotten the time. As she ran through the corridors on her way to the running track, she bumped into Mr Sebele. "Careful, 'Pheidippides!'" said Mr Sebele. "I was just coming to find you. Hurry up or we'll start the battle without you!" He laughed at his own little joke.

Mr Sebele was a good coach, but he did have a high opinion of himself. He thought he was very clever and funny. He liked to use big words. This one was clearly a name; it sounded like 'Fydipedees'. Who was that?

"I'm sorry, sir," said Kgatlhanang. She began to explain about the history project, but he interrupted her.

"Not to worry, Kgatlhanang. Just hurry over to the track. They're waiting to start your race."

Kgatlhanang did as she was told. She had no time to ask who Pheidippides was.

Kgatlhanang won her race. She won all her races that afternoon. They were practising for the inter-school sports at the weekend. Mr Sebele did not say much, but Kgatlhanang could tell he was pleased. So was she. As she ran through Kanye on her way home, she was thinking about the inter-school sports day. How she hoped she would win against the Kweneng Zone runners on Saturday!

When she reached the bush, Kgatlhanang remembered the
mysterious runner from the night before. Who was she?
Where had she come from? Kgatlhanang wondered if she
would see the girl again. She passed two old women who
were walking back to Kanye, carrying firewood on their
heads. She waved to a little boy who was driving some goats
home. But after that, she was alone in the bush.

Kgatlhanang saw no one else until she reached the long,
narrow hill. She ran up the track at the end of the hill, then
stopped in surprise. There in front of her was the runner. The
girl looked back over her shoulder at Kgatlhanang. Again
Kgatlhanang saw the frightened look on the girl's face.
Suddenly, the girl cried out, stumbled and fell. Kgatlhanang
ran up to her.

"Are you all right?" she asked.

"I twisted my ankle as I fell," said the girl. "I stood on a thorn." Her voice and her face showed that she was in pain. Bravely, she pulled the thorn out of her foot. It was a long thorn, as sharp as a needle. Once it had been white, but now it was red with blood from the girl's foot.

The girl tried to stand up, but cried out as she put her weight on her injured ankle. She fell again, with an unhappy cry. Her ankle was obviously very painful. Kgatlhanang had twisted her own ankle in the past, so she knew how much it hurt. But the girl was not only in pain, she was also terribly upset. Was something else troubling her?

"Does it hurt a lot? Can I help you?" asked Kgatlhanang, kneeling down beside the girl.

"Yes," replied the girl. She looked at Kgatlhanang. "I'll have to trust you." This seemed a strange thing to say, but the girl began to explain. "They are here. We met them at Losabanyana. Although we did our best, it was no good." Kgatlhanang could see the girl was trying not to cry. Her voice shook with sorrow as she spoke. "Makaba is dead. I must get a message to my cousin, Tebogo. My mother has sent me because Tebogo will know what to do."

Kgatlhanang did not really understand what the girl was saying, but she could see how upset she was. Perhaps Makaba was one of her relatives. *Makaba* ... Kgatlhanang was sure she had heard that name before, but she could not

remember where. She took off her rucksack and put it down.

"Can you walk, if you lean on me?" she said to the girl. But the girl shook her head impatiently.

"There is no time," said the girl. "If you want to help, you must take the message to Tebogo. Run now, as fast as you can. Run to the end of the hilltop and take the path by the tree with the broken branch. Follow the path down and into the valley. Tebogo will be waiting at the pool. Show him this, to prove you come from me. My name is Sentle." She took the bracelet off her wrist. It was made of leather and ostrich shell beads. Kgatlhanang thought it was very beautiful. Sentle put the bracelet onto Kgatlhanang's wrist and said, "Tell him Makaba is dead." Sentle was almost crying. " Poor Tebogo. What terrible news! But he will know what to do; he will be brave."

Then she broke down and began to cry wildly.
Kgatlhanang tried to comfort her.

"Please don't cry, Sentle. It's all right. Don't cry," she
said, but it was no use. Kgatlhanang sighed. She felt that the
only way to comfort Sentle was to do what she asked. She
stood up and looked down at the unhappy girl for a second,
then she ran off.

Crunch, crunch, crunch, crunch ... the rhythm of her
running shoes was faster than ever. Dust flew up from her
heels as she raced along. For some strange reason,
Kgatlhanang shared Sentle's unhappiness. She was filled
with the need for speed. Although she did not know why, she
felt this was the most important race of her life.

The end of the hilltop was soon in sight. Kgatlhanang did
not remember seeing a tree there at the side of the track
before. She thought she usually ran past an old, dead stump.
But there was a tree; it was tall and had a broken branch.
This branch pointed, like a sign post, down a narrow path off
the side of the track. Kgatlhanang took this path. Branches
brushed against her hair and scratched her arms and legs, but
she ran on. She ran down into the valley and raced along the
path. Would she find a pool there? She had never seen a pool
in the valley. She knew there was a dry, empty hollow. This
sometimes filled with water after the rains, but it had not
rained for a long time.

The sun was low in the sky. Kgatlhanang's shadow was a
giant running along beside her. The girl and her shadow ran
together, faster and faster, through the bush. Kgatlhanang's

breath came out in gasps. Through the bushes ahead she saw something bright. It was the pool. It shone like a new coin in the evening sunlight. Kgatlhanang crashed through the last bushes and reached the water.

A tall figure was standing like a statue beside the pool. It was a young man with a long spear in his hand. Kgatlhanang gasped for breath.

"Are you Tebogo?" she asked the young man. He nodded his head. Kgatlhanang gasped out her message. "I come to you from Sentle. She fell and hurt her ankle on her way here. I have her bracelet to prove I come from her. Her message is this. *They* came and Sentle's people met them at Losabanyana. I'm sorry, Makaba is dead. Sentle said you would know what to do."

Kgatlhanang felt rather silly. She did not really understand her message. She wished the young man would say something. At last he spoke.

"I watched you run along the hilltop and through the valley. You ran very fast and you were not followed, which is good. You have Sentle's bracelet and I see in your eyes that you speak the truth, although you do not understand it." He paused and sighed. "Makaba is dead! Then I must run south to our friends, the English traders. They have horses and guns. They can help us." He paused again. His face looked very sad and very angry. "Tell Sentle I understand her message and I know what to do." He smiled at Kgatlhanang for a moment. Then he turned and ran into the bush. In a few seconds, he was out of sight.

The sun had disappeared behind one of the hills. The pool was silent and dark at Kgatlhanang's feet. She shivered. She did not understand what Tebogo had said about horses and guns. Once again, she began to run, more slowly this time. She went back through the valley, up the path and along the hilltop. It was almost dark by the time she reached her rucksack. Sentle had disappeared.

Kgatlhanang looked all around and called Sentle's name as loudly as she could. There was no reply. Maybe somebody had found Sentle and taken her home. Suddenly Kgatlhanang was angry. Sentle had not even waited, or left a note to say where she lived. Kgatlhanang put on her rucksack and started to walk home. She knew her way and she was not afraid of the dark, but she was tired. She had run far enough for one day.

It was very late when Kgatlhanang arrived home. Her
mother, who had been worried, spoke angrily.

"Where have you been until this time? Kgatlhanang, you
must get home earlier than this. I was afraid something had
happened to you."

Kgatlhanang began to explain, but her mother was too
busy to listen properly. There was just time for a wash before
the evening meal. Then there was homework to do. It took
rather a long time because she kept thinking about Sentle and
Tebogo. At last she finished. She closed her books with a
yawn and went to bed.

All through the next morning's lessons, Kgatlhanang
thought about Sentle and Tebogo. At lunchtime, she stayed in
the classroom again to work on the history display. Leatile
was there. He smiled at her across the classroom.

"See you later," he whispered as loudly as he dared. He pretended to bounce a ball and nodded towards the playing field. He had a basketball practice in the afternoon and Kgatlhanang would see him after that. She nodded happily at him. Then she looked at the work Mrs Maswabe had given her.

Some of the class had written accounts of events from the Kololo migration. Mrs Maswabe had told them to write the accounts as if they were newspaper articles. She had given some of these 'newspaper articles' to Kgatlhanang to stick onto coloured paper. Kgatlhanang placed the first article on the coloured paper, very carefully. When she looked at the article itself, she saw that it had been written by Leatile. Smiling, she read the article. It was good; Leatile had done

his research well. But Kgatlhanang's eyes opened wide with surprise. The words seemed to jump off the paper at her. She read the article all the way through, then she read it again, because she could not believe her eyes. But there was no mistake; the article was very clear.

BATTLE AT LOSABANYANA

The Kololo won a terrible victory at Losabanyana near Kanye yesterday. The Ngwaketse fought bravely but they could not win against the mighty Kololo. The Ngwaketse were defeated. The Ngwaketse chief, Makaba, was killed in the battle. The Kololo chief, Sebetwane, was seriously wounded in the chest by a spear. Many men from both armies were killed.

The article was dated 7 August, 1826. She was sure Leatile's research was correct. But the place and Makaba's name; were they just coincidences? Last evening, Sentle had spoken about these things as if they had just happened. Kgatlhanang had not understood everything then, but suddenly Sentle's words had a new meaning. Kgatlhanang's heart was beating fast as she read Leatile's second article. This was dated 18 August, 1826.

KOLOLO DEFEATED IN DAWN ATTACK

The Kololo were defeated yesterday in a surprise attack by the Ngwaketse. Many Kololo were killed. Their settlement in the hills to the east of Kanye was burnt to the ground. The new Ngwatketse chief, Sebego, was helped by Englishmen with horses and guns. These guns won the battle for the Ngwatketse. The Kololo were afraid of the guns and ran away. They left behind large herds of cattle they had captured from the Ngwaketse people.

The Kololo were very badly prepared for the battle. Their chief, Sebetwane, was still recovering from a wound received at the battle of Losabanya. The Ngwaketse were able to act quickly and surprise the Kololo. A young Ngwaketse warrior, called Tebogo, took the news to the Englishmen. After the Battle of Losabanya, Tebogo ran a great distance, about 42 kilometres, to bring the help of the Englishmen. Tebogo's race against time saved the Ngwaketse.

Kgatlhanang stared at the pieces of paper in front of her. She thought carefully and remembered everything that had happened the previous evening. But she was no longer sure if it *was* the previous evening. Maybe she was remembering an evening which had happened long ago. Somehow, she had gone back in time, to an evening over 160 years ago.

For a moment, she thought she must be mad. Surely she had imagined everything! Then she felt something on her wrist. Looking down, she saw Sentle's bracelet. She took it off and looked at it more closely. Yes, it was real. But now she noticed that the leather looked thin and tired. The ostrich shell beads were dull and worn. The bracelet looked very old.

Kgatlhanang stood up suddenly. She wanted to be in the fresh air, where she could think. She walked into the corridor and, once again, bumped into Mr Sebele.

"Hey, 'Pheidippides!'" he said. "What's the matter? Can't you see where you're going?"

"Mr Sebele, who is Pheidippides?" asked Kgatlhanang, although her mind was far away.

"He was a long distance runner, like yourself. He lived in ancient Greece. He ran from Athens to Sparta to get help before the Battle of Marathon, which the Greeks fought against the Persians. After the battle, he ran back to Athens to tell everyone the news of the victory. The modern marathon race is named after his achievement."

Kgatlhanang was silent and she smiled. Pheidippides was a good name for all three of them – Sentle, Tebogo and her.

Between them, they had passed on the news of one battle and brought help for another. Could Sentle and Tebogo have succeeded without her? No; that was why she had been sent back in time. She had been needed. And *she* had needed all her strength and skill as a runner. Kgatlhanang felt very happy. The race on Saturday would be easy. All her races would be easy in future. She had already run the most important race of her life.

Glossary

account	Description of an event.
achievement	Successful task or piece of work.
clipboard	Hand-held board on which papers are pinned.
contain	To hold within.
ancestors	Members of the family who lived long ago.
bracelet	Ornament worn on the wrist.
click	To make a small, sharp noise.
decorate	To make something pleasing to look at.
delighted	Very pleased.
display	(To make) a collection of things to look at.
expect	To believe something will happen.
glow	To shine.
frown	To have an angry expression.
gasp	To breathe out quickly in surprise or after exercise.
grit	Small pieces of stone and earth.
look forward to	To think happily about some thing that is going to happen.
impossible	Something that cannot be.
migrate	To leave one place and move elsewhere.
puzzled	Unable to understand.
reception	Place where visitors are received.
rucksack	Bag carried on the back with straps for the shoulders.

shiver	To move one's arms and legs slightly when cold or afraid.
sink (sank)	To move downwards into or through something.
slender	Slim.
sole	Underneath part of a foot or shoe.
stall	small shop.
steep	Land that gains or loses height over a short distance.
stopwatch	Small clock for timing events precisely.
straight	Having no bends or corners.
stretch	To extend.
stumble	To trip, almost to fall.
stump	Base that remains of a tree which has been cut down.
surprise	Feeling of wonder.
tease	To say things about someone in a playful manner.
terror	Fear.
twist	To turn or bend.
wave	To raise one's hand in greeting.
whistle	To make a loud, high pitched noise by blowing air through a small space.

Questions and activities

1   How did Kgatlhanang travel to school every morning?
2   Which race did Kgatlhanang win at the beginning of the story?
3   What three things did Kgatlhanang's rucksack contain?
4   Write out and complete these sentences, selecting the correct words from those given below:

> Kgatlhanang ran through _____ in the evening. She was faster than the_____ but the _____were faster than she was.

> *minibuses   Kanye   donkey carts*

5   How had Kgatlhanang felt the first time she had run home from school?
6   What were Kgatlhanang's plans for her running in the future, after she left school?
7   Here is a map showing the start of Kgatlhanang's journey home. Draw a pencil line on the map to show the route she will take during this part of the journey.

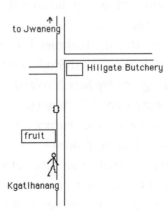

8   Which bird did Kgatlhanang hear when she reached the bush?

9   Why does the author describe the track as being 'like a snake'?

10   Which sport did Leatile play?

11   Why did Kgatlhanang look forward to reaching the top of the long narrow hill?

12   What surprised Kgatlhanang about the other girl's running?

13   What surprised Kgatlhanang when she reached the edge of the hilltop?

14   What did Leatile call Kgatlhanang when he saw her the next day?

15   Briefly describe the Social Studies project they were working on. Mention the subject matter and the kind of work produced.

16   What was the name of Kgatlhanang's coach?

17   On the second evening, Sentle fell. Why?

18   What was Kgatlhanang given to prove to Tebogo that she has been sent by Sentle?

19   What did Tebogo say he would do when he received Sentle's message?

20   The day after she had met Tebogo, Kgatlhanang worked on the Social Studies project again. What task was she given by Mrs Maswabe?

21   What were Leatile's 'newspaper articles' about?

22   Why did the articles surprise Kgatlhanang?

23   Who was Pheidippiddes?

24   How did the marathon race get its name?

25   How did Kgatlhanang explain to herself the events of the evening when she met Sentle and Tebogo?

Match up the following phrases from the text with their meanings, which are listed on page 36.

Phrases

She got a lift to Kanye every morning ...

She wanted to run for Botswana ...

She knew every twist and turn of the track ...

She didn't mind ...

It felt good to stretch her legs ...

Kgatlhanang decided to catch up with her and find out ...

Kgatlhanang did as she was told ...

Then she broke down ...

A tall figure was standing like a statue ...

The words seemed to jump off the paper at her ...

Meanings

Kgatlhanang thought she would run quickly and reach the other girl so that she could discover who she was.

Kgatlhanang obeyed.

She ran that way so often that she knew the route very well.

She travelled to Kanye in her neighbour's vehicle every day.

She hoped she would be a good enough runner to be picked for the Botswana team.

After that, she couldn't control her emotions any more.

She didn't object.

She enjoyed taking longer strides.

The writing was so interesting she couldn't concentrate on anything else.

There was a tall person who didn't move at all.

Further analysis of the text.

1 Explain the significance of Kgatlhanang's friends' remark, "At the speed you're going you'll get to tomorrow before us."

2 Re-read the paragraghs on pages 21-22, beginning, "The end of the hilltop was soon in sight," and ending, "Kgatlhanang crashed through the last bushes and reached the water." What indications are there that Kgatlhanang had left her own time and was running in the past?

3 Write a brief description of *either* Leatile *or* Mr Sebele.

Further activities

1 Find out what you can about the Kololo people. Write an
   account of their migration. Illustrate your account with a
   route map.

2 Choose any historical event that you have learnt about in
   Social Studies. Imagine that you were there as a
   journalist. Write an article about the event for your
   newspaper *The Botswana Times.*

3 Find out more about the modern Olympic Games. Write
   an article about them for the school magazine. Include the
   following facts:

   What is the world record at the moment for the Women's
   3000 metres race? Who holds this record?

   What is the distance of the marathon race? Who won the
   women's marathon at the last Olympic Games?

4 Do you think it is possible to 'travel in time' as
   Kgatlhanang did? Write a story about someone who
   travelled in time either into the past, or into the future.